# Naughty Spot! It's dinner time. Where can he be?

# Is he behind the door?

# Is he inside the clock?

# Is he in the piano?

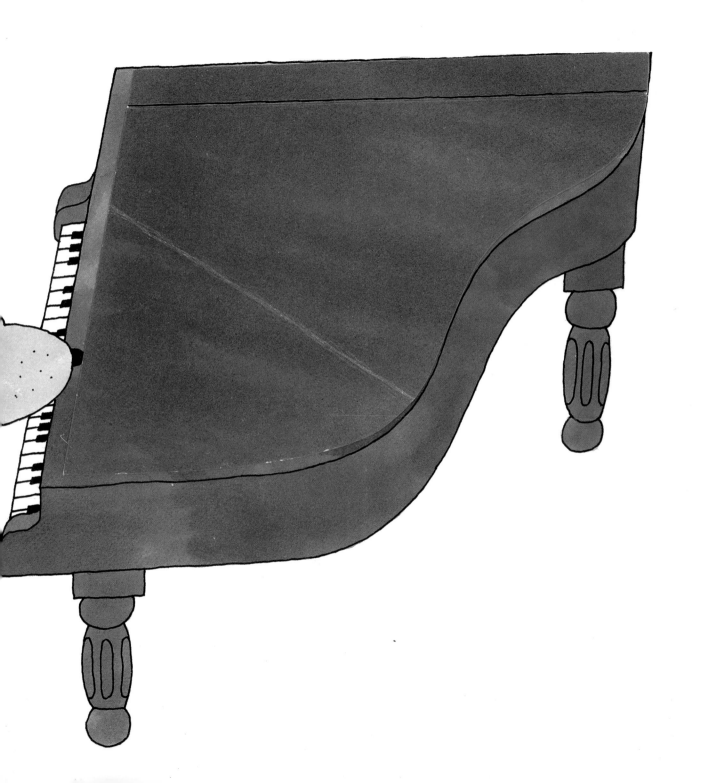

# Is he under the stairs?

# Is he
# in the wardrobe?

# Is he under the bed?

# Is he
# in the
# box?

# There's Spot!

## He's under the rug.